Lenny and Wilbur
Published in the UK & Ireland by Alanna Max
38 Oakfield Road, London N4 4NL

First published in Paperback in 2021
Lenny and Wilbur © 2019 Alanna Max
Text and illustrations copyright © 2019 Ken Wilson-Max

Author and Illustrator Ken Wilson-Max
www.kenwilsonmax.com

First published in Hardback in 2019
First published in Big Book in 2021

British Library Cataloguing in Publication Data available on request

Illustrated with acrylic
Typeset in KGHappy

www.AlannaMax.com

ISBN 978-1-907825-24-8 HB
ISBN 978-1-907825-41-5 PB
ISBN 978-1-907825-42-2 Big Book

Printed in China

123456789

Lenny and Wilbur

Ken Wilson-Max

Alanna Max

Lenny and Wilbur are
the best of friends.

**Best friends
have fun together!**

"It's Wilbur's bath day today!
Ask him to sit." Mummy says.

"Sit!" says Lenny.
Wilbur sits.

"First, some warm water
to wet his fur."

"Then, shampoo
to wash it clean."
says Mummy.

Wilbur shakes.
Lenny giggles.
Best friends
laugh together!

Lenny rubs
Wilbur's tummy
and brushes
his fur.

Wilbur gets a treat.
"Good doggy!" says Mummy.
"Good doggy!" says Lenny.

Best friends eat together
"Good boy, Lenny!" says Mummy.
"Good boy, Wilbur!" says Lenny.

Wilbur tickles Lenny's ear.
Is it time for a song?

Old McDonald had a farm
Hee-hi hee-hi ho!

And on that farm he had a dog
Hee-hi hee-hi ho!

With a Woof Woof here
And a Woof Woof there

Here a Woof, there a Woof
Everywhere a Woof Woof!

Old McDonald had a farm
Hee-hi hee-hi ho!

When they are finally tired,
best friends rest together.